"*Mittman . . . does sweet historical romance to perfection.*"
—Publishers Weekly

"*Stephanie Mittman might very well become the standard against which all future Americana romance is judged!*"
—Affaire de Coeur

chanted fabric they wrought enfolded them in a bond that grew stronger with each passing day.

She smiled back at him, and she was rewarded with the satisfaction she found in his warm gaze.

Alasdair made a rude noise. "Och, dinna swoon into each other's arms in front of me, if ye please. Have the decency to conduct yer lovers' looks when I'm no about."

"Hello, Alasdair," Griffin said with a wink to Cicely.

"He speaks," Alasdair said to Honeysett as he picked the puppy up in his arms. He scratched behind floppy ears. "Perhaps we're no forgotten after all, my bonny wee one."

Honeysett smiled and tried to lick the ghost's face, but his pink tongue passed right through. It didn't seem to bother the puppy a bit.

Cicely remembered why she'd come. "I brought your noon meal. You forgot it again."

"Mayhap I didn't forget at all," Griffin said, lifting her hand to press a kiss to her fingertips. "Mayhap I only wanted your sweet company."

Alasdair made another rude noise.

Reluctantly, Cicely withdrew her hand from Griffin's to try to concentrate on the other purpose of her trip out here. "Alasdair has most graciously offered to let us move into the abbey."

Griffin looked at Alasdair, who suddenly found scratching Honeysett's ears a task that required all his attention. To Cicely's surprise, she thought she saw a faint pink tint Alasdair's translucent face.

"Gracious, indeed," Griffin said dryly. "And what brought about this unexpected generosity?"

Alasdair cleared his throat. "'Tis only that it dinna seem proper to have Cicely's weans conceived any-where but the manor house."

"I agree." Griffin accorded Alasdair a small bow. "Thank you."

The civility her two favorite males were showing each other pleased Cicely, but she decided it was best not to put a strain on it by keeping them together for long. She handed Griffin his cloth-wrapped meal and a crockery jar of ale. "I'd best return to my work and leave you to yours."

At that moment, a horse galloped into view, bearing a well-dressed rider. Rapidly, he drew near enough for Cicely to identify the rider. "Randolph."

"They freed him until the House of Lords convenes," Griffin said.

She slipped her hand into his, and he gave her an encouraging little squeeze.

"Randolph has made a lot of enemies," he said. "Many of them are now my allies. The lords will fine him, but they'll leave him his freedom. The Tyrrell titles, land, and wealth will also remain his."

She looked up at him. "You mean your plan failed?"

He shook his head. "They'll strip away his greater power. His important contacts in government and society will fade away. 'Tis the power he feeds on. It's what makes him truly dangerous. I knew they'd never go so far as to try to revoke the titles." He shrugged. "They have only my word that he's an impostor, and what is the word of a second son? Possession has, as always, the greater weight of the law. Quickly, now go back to the house."

Unwilling to desert her husband in a confrontation with his enemy, Cicely remained where she was. Before Griffin could repeat his order, Randolph reined in his horse, facing them from the road. The horse danced restively under his heavy-handed command.

He wore no wig today. Instead, his own thin grayish

brown hair hung in lank clumps to his shoulders. His bloodshot eyes glared at them, and under them Cicely noticed dark half circles. His magnificently embroidered suit of clothes was rumpled and stained.

Cicely felt Griffin's hand pushing her in the direction of the house, but she resisted.

"So," Randolph said, glancing at Alasdair, "this is the vaunted ghost of Cranwick Abbey. The demon that terrorized armed dragoons. A Scotsman."

Alasdair bridled. "Keep a respectful tone in yer mouth when ye say that word. 'Tis no a thing ye can even aspire to, Englishman."

"Why aren't you turning into a death's-head or something?" Cicely whispered out of the side of her mouth.

"I canna do that. He's no on the manor," Alasdair replied.

Strangely enough, Randolph already seemed to have forgotten Alasdair. His eyes were focused on Griffin with a mad intensity. "All these years you've been working to bring me down, haven't you? Going behind my back. Conspiring with my enemies." His voice rose higher and higher. "You'd love to see me fall! I'm already receiving letters from London. *Excuses!* Excuses from small-minded men who call themselves lords. They seek to distance themselves from me."

He pointed a bare white finger at Griffin. "You! You've done this. Well, it won't work. I'm the duke of Marwood!"

"No," Griffin said. "You're not."

Randolph's unshaven face twisted with savage hatred. "I *am* the duke of Marwood. I am! That's all I have. *You* had the love of the only father I knew. *You* had a beautiful mother who adored you—not that bitter, old harridan who stole me, not the bird-witted peasant who bore me.

You were wanted. I was merely tolerated. So I took what I could."

He sliced an arm through the air. "I stole your birthright from under the noses of everyone. And you were left with what I'd had for years—nothing. I liked that. I liked hurting you. I liked the thought of you dead. I used to picture myself at your funeral. Oh, I'd look so grieved, while all along I'd be rejoicing inside. Free at last!"

Cicely watched Randolph with growing alarm. His words were coming faster, tumbling out in growing agitation. Though Griffin appeared to stand calmly beside her, she felt the tension humming through him.

"But you've managed to evade my traps," Randolph ranted on. "And now . . . My God, now you're bloody happy again! Nothing but a farmer on some Sussex dunghill, and you're happy."

Out of the corner of her eye, Cicely glimpsed a hare hopping and nibbling, hopping and nibbling. Then a motion from Randolph captured her full attention. From the concealment of his coat, he whipped out a pistol. He pointed it straight at Cicely's heart.

"If I cannot have happiness, Griffin, neither shall you!" he cried.

Griffin shoved Cicely down as he flung himself in front of her. As she fell, she heard the explosion from the pistol and Griffin's grunt of pain.

Alasdair shouted with alarm as Honeysett spotted the hare and leaped from his arms in pursuit.

The frightened hare dashed out into the road, between the feet of Randolph's nervous mount. With a shrill scream, the horse reared wildly, tumbling Randolph to the ground.

Honeysett followed the hare in determined pursuit, right into danger of being trampled.

"No!" Alasdair cried and flew after him, plucking the pup to safety just as iron-shod hooves crashed down.

Cicely scrambled over to where Griffin sat holding his shoulder. Blood seeped through his fingers.

"It isn't bad," he said through gritted teeth. "Looks much worse than it is." He managed a smile to reassure her. "Hurts like the devil, though."

They got to their feet and went to examine Randolph's still form. His head lay at a peculiar angle. A trickle of blood had escaped the corner of his mouth, and his unblinking eyes stared up at the sky. Griffin felt for a pulse, then shook his head.

"I feel odd," Alasdair said.

They turned to see a strange glow forming around him.

"Alasdair," Cicely cried as she ran to him. "You've left Cranwick land. You crossed the boundary!" Dear God, the book had said that if he crossed the boundary his soul would be lost forever.

"I know, lass," he said softly. "But I couldna verra well let the pup die. He's been my friend."

To their astonishment a small glittering sliver appeared in the air beside him. It grew and materialized into a lovely woman dressed all in green.

"Alasdair Andrew MacNab," she said, her voice like music, "you have performed an act of sacrificial kindness. Knowing the dire consequences, you left the manor anyway, that you might save this small creature from harm." She offered Alasdair her hand. He eyed it with distrust, and she smiled. "Come. The ban is lifted. You have earned your peace."

He took her hand. They began to fade.

Cicely smiled through her tears. "Good-bye, Alasdair." She rejoiced for him, but she sorrowed for herself. She would sorely miss her friend.

Although she could scarcely distinguish him now from the hedge shrubs behind him, she saw him raise his hand. "Good-bye, sweet Cicely." Then they were no more than a glimmer, and finally even that vanished.

Griffin gathered her into his arms. "It's what he wanted, sweetheart."

She nodded, tasting the salt of her tears. "I'll miss him."

They turned and slowly walked toward the manor, their arms around each other's waist. Honeysett loped along beside them.

Then she heard it, Alasdair's voice drifting back on the bright air.

"Mary! Mary, love, is it really you?"

Epilogue

"*Another gift has arrived* for Master Alexander, Your Grace," Bromage the butler intoned, holding out a silver tray bearing a small package.

Sitting at his desk in the library at Cranwick Abbey, Griffin set aside his quill, deciding to take a small break from the small mountain of correspondence that required his attention. In the almost two years since Randolph's death, Griffin had developed and maintained a powerful network of allies and spies. Little occurred in the kingdom that the eighth duke of Marwood did not soon learn.

"Thank you, Bromage," he said, accepting the handsomely wrapped present. Glancing at the small cream-colored card affixed, he recognized the embossed ducal crest and smiled. The duke of Newcastle had become more than an ally. It saddened Griffin to think of Thomas's failing health.

"Have you seen Lady Marwood?" Griffin asked Bromage.

"I believe she is in the nursery, Your Grace."

Which was where Griffin found her several minutes later, giving her undivided attention to their month-old son, Alexander. She stood by a window, softly singing a lullaby to the baby she held in her arms. He quietly observed and smiled as a deep pride filled him. His beautiful, intelligent wife had given him an exceptionally bright son, complete with chestnut hair and brandy brown eyes.

Griffin felt a light touch on his shoulder. He turned around to find Susan and Ann, Cicely's younger sisters, smiling up at him. He stepped aside and they entered the nursery chamber, eager, as usual, to hold and spoil their infant nephew.

As Cicely had predicted, the letters she had written Susan and Ann had been kept from them by their father, who sought to disaffect them from their sister, lest she inform them of Edmund's preference for men, about which he had known all along. The fellow had received no opportunity to cause further trouble, however. Shortly after receiving Griffin's letter setting out his desire to provide for Cicely's sisters, their father had expired over a losing hand of cards. The doctor had declared seizure of the heart.

"Let me hold him, please," Ann wheedled.

"No, me, please, Cicely. Ann held him this morning."

Cicely's lips curved in a gentle smile that reminded Griffin of every masterpiece he'd ever seen of the Madonna. "He's asleep now," she said softly, "so you both must wait until later." She took the babe to his satin-draped cradle, placing him inside with the greatest care. "Come," she whispered to her sisters. Her silk skirts rustled as she moved away. Instantly Alexander's nursemaid swept forward to hover over the cradle until she'd satisfied herself that all was well with the child.

Griffin did not miss the sudden light in Cicely's eyes when she saw him standing just inside the nursery door, and the joy he took in that sight burned like a white flame within him.

"What brings you to your son's nursery, my lord?" she asked in a gay, soft voice, walking confidently into his arms.

He held her close to him. "Must a man have a reason to wish to see his son? Or his lovely wife?"

She smiled up at him. "No, never." She stood on her tiptoes and kissed him.

He heard her sisters' giggles, smothered behind their hands.

"Ladies do not giggle," Cicely told them firmly in a low voice. "'Tis *trés gauche*."

They nodded demurely as they hastened from the nursery. Seconds later there was a burst of feminine laughter in the hall.

Griffin and Cicely shared an amused look. Well, it was good to hear them so happy.

He took her hand and led her out into the hall. "Thomas sent a gift for Alexander." He set the package in her palm.

She looked thoughtful for a moment. "He's been a good friend. I wish that he were feeling better." Then she tugged his hand. "The weather is mild. Let's go to the roof."

He allowed her to tow him toward the back stairway. "Very well. Is the packing finished? You know we must leave for Ashton no later than tomorrow morning."

"Yes, yes, and then on to London next month. All is ready."

Concerned that she might weary of the seasonal moves, he asked, "Does it make you unhappy?"

She laughed. "No, silly. I enjoy all our travels." Her eyes twinkled with mischief as she leaned closer to confide, "I love being married to an important man."

He grinned as he drew her to him and ran his hands up and down her back. "Would you love me if I were only a farmer?"

"I *have* loved you as only a farmer, in case you've forgotten. I would love you if you were naught but a gypsy or a swineherd." She feigned a frown. "Well, perhaps not a swineherd."

Now it was his turn to laugh, and he waltzed her to the staircase, reveling in her intoxicating laughter.

They climbed up to the banqueting tower, where he held her in his arms as they looked out over the rich, green land.

"Once you wanted adventure," he said.

"And now I have it. My life is filled with adventure."

"It is?"

Cicely chuckled. "Certainly. Perhaps nothing about which a novel will ever be written, but eminently satisfying nonetheless."

Yes, eminently satisfying, Griffin agreed silently. "I'm glad."

She sighed contentedly. "And to think, without Alasdair, we might never have met."

As if by some unspoken agreement, they both turned to search out that lone headstone. Every day since the incident at the manor's boundary, when Randolph had shot Griffin, and Alasdair had saved Honeysett, fresh flowers were placed on Alasdair's grave, and rose plants now grew where once nettles had thrived.

"I take comfort in believing he found Mary again," Cicely said quietly.

Griffin pressed a kiss to the crown of her head. He was a fortunate man. After years of danger and struggle, he'd finally found a place in the world he could call his own—in the tender heart of this extraordinary woman.

After all this time, she still believed in magic.

And after his time with her, so did he.

Let HarperMonogram Sweep You Away!

Sooner or Later by Debbie Macomber
Twelve million copies of her books in print. Letty Madden asks a soldier of fortune to help her find her brother in Central America, but Murphy's price is high—one night with the demure postmistress. Letty accepts and Murphy realizes that protecting his heart may prove to be his most difficult mission of all.

A Hidden Magic by Terri Lynn Wilhelm
Ghost romance. When Cicely Honeysett sells Griffin Tyrrell her family's estate, she forgets to tell him about the mischievous ghost that has made Cranwick Abbey his own. At odds with the unwelcoming spirit, Griffin yearns for Cicely—a heavenly creature who will share his bed instead of trying to chase him from it.

Queen of My Heart by Donna Valentino
Time travel romance. Dante Trevani escapes from an unwanted betrothal in Tudor England by traveling through time to 19th-century Arizona and beautiful Gloriana Carlisle. When he realizes his fiancée is destined to be the Queen of England, Dante must choose between returning to the past or staying with the queen of his heart.

Montana Morning by Jill Limber
Debut novel. To find a husband and claim her family's ranch in the Montana Territory, Katherine Holman marries Wes Merrick and saves him from the hangman's noose. Wes refuses to ride off into the sunset, however, and instead tries to turn a marriage of convenience into a match made in heaven.

And in case you missed last month's selections . . .

Chances Are by Robin Lee Hatcher
Over three million copies of her books in print. Her young daughter's illness forces traveling actress Faith Butler to take a job at the Jagged R Ranch working for Drake Rutledge. Passions rise when the beautiful thespian is drawn to her rugged employer and the forbidden pleasure of his touch.

Mystic Moon by Patricia Simpson

"One of the premier writers of supernatural romance."—Romantic Times. A brush with death changes Carter Greyson's life and irrevocably links him to an endangered Indian tribe. Dr. Arielle Scott, who is intrigued by the mysterious Carter, shares this destiny—a destiny that will lead them both to the magic of lasting love.

Just a Miracle by Zita Christian

When dashing Jake Darrow brings his medicine show to Coventry, Montana, pharmacist Brenna McAuley wants nothing to do with him. But it's only a matter of time before Brenna discovers that romance is just what the doctor ordered.

Raven's Bride by Lynn Kerstan

When Glenys Shea robbed the reclusive Earl of Ravensby, she never expected to steal his heart instead of his gold. Now the earl's prisoner, the charming thief must prove her innocence—and her love.

Harper Monogram

Escape to Romance
and
WIN A YEAR OF ROMANCE!

Ten lucky winners will receive a free year of romance—*more than 30 free books*. Every book HarperMonogram publishes in 1997 will be delivered directly to your doorstep if you are one of the ten winners drawn at random.

RULES: To enter, send your name, address, and daytime telephone number to the ESCAPE TO ROMANCE CONTEST, HarperPaperbacks, 10 East 53rd Street, New York, NY 10022. No purchase necessary. This contest is open to U.S. residents 18 years or older, except employees (and their families) of HarperPaperbacks/HarperCollins and their agencies, affiliates, and subsidiaries. Entries must be received by October 31, 1996. HarperPaperbacks is not responsible for late, lost, incomplete, or misdirected mail. Winners will be selected in a random drawing on or about November 15, 1996 and notified by mail. All entries become the property of HarperPaperbacks and will not be returned or acknowledged. Entry constitutes permission to use winner's name, home town, and likeness for promotional purposes on behalf of HarperPaperbacks. Winners must sign Affidavit of Eligiblity, Assignment, and Release within 10 days of notification. Approximate retail value of each prize $250.

All federal, state, and local laws and regulations apply. Void where prohibited. Applicable taxes are the sole responsiblity of the winners. Prizes are not exchangeable or transferable. No substitutions of prizes except at the discretion of HarperPaperbacks. For a list of winners send a self-addressed, stamped envelope to the address above after January 1, 1997.

Harper
Monogram